JUDY MOODY AND FRIENDS

April Fools', Mr. Todd!

Megan McDonald

illustrated by Erwin Madrid

based on the characters
created by Peter H. Reynolds

CANDLEWICK PRESS

For Merlin Vaughan

M. M.

For Silvano Madrid

E. M.

Text copyright © 2017 by Megan McDonald
Illustrations copyright © 2017 by Peter H. Reynolds
Judy Moody font copyright © 2003 by Peter H. Reynolds

First edition 2017

Library of Congress Catalog Card Number pending
ISBN 978-0-7636-8200-2 (hardcover)
ISBN 978-0-7636-8201-9 (paperback)

16 17 18 19 20 21 TLF 10 9 8 7 6 5 4 3 2 1

Printed in Dongguan, Guangdong, China

MIX
Paper from
responsible sources
FSC® C104723
FSC
www.fsc.org

This book was typeset in ITC Stone Informal.
The illustrations were created digitally.

Candlewick Press
99 Dover Street
Somerville, Massachusetts 02144

visit us at www.candlewick.com

CONTENTS

CHAPTER 1
April Fish and Spaghetti Trees

Mr. Todd was the boss of Class 3T.
As in, WBT: World's Best Teacher.
He wore wacky ties (penguins). He
made up goofy songs on the guitar
("Guinea Pigs Are Not Pigs"). He liked
treasure hunts (for spelling words).
The inchworm crayon was his favorite
color (spring green). And he had the
best sticker collection in all of Virginia
Dare School (*Hot Dog with Awesome
Sauce!*).

Today Mr. Todd was changing his bulletin board. Down with snowflakes. Up with spring!

"Who knows what special days are coming up in April?" Mr. Todd asked.

Hands shot up. "Earth Day!" "Tax Day!" "Peanut-Butter-and-Jelly Day!"

"Blah-Blah-Blah Day," said Frank Pearl. The class got quiet.

"What?" said Frank. "It's a real thing. April seventeenth. Look it up."

Mr. Todd checked his calendar and read out, "Blah-Blah-Blah Day is a day to get things done that you've put off."

"Blah," said Judy. Class 3T cracked up.

"I'm thinking of another special day," said Mr. Todd, "that falls on the first of the month."

"My birthday!" Judy squealed, but nobody heard her. They were all shouting, "April Fools' Day!"

"And what happens on April Fools' Day?" asked Mr. Todd.

"Funny stuff!" "Pranks!" "Jokes!"

"That's right," said Mr. Todd. "Has anybody ever heard of spaghetti trees?"

"Spaghetti doesn't grow on *trees*," said Jessica Finch.

"True, but one April Fools' Day years ago, a news program in England reported that it was a good year for growing spaghetti.

They even showed pictures of trees with spaghetti hanging from the branches."

"No way!" "Cuckoo!" "For real?"

"People believed the report. They called the TV station to find out where they could get spaghetti-tree seeds. Everybody wanted one."

Class 3T laughed their pants off.

"Nobody really knows how April Fools' Day started," said Mr. Todd, "but it's been around for hundreds of years. In France and Italy, they call it April Fish Day."

"April Fish Day? Is that when you skip school to go fishing?" asked Rocky.

"No," said Mr. Todd. "That's when you tape a picture of a fish onto somebody's back, and see how long it takes them to figure it out."

"Rare!" said Judy.

"In India, each spring they hold a festival called Holi. During Holi, people paint

their faces bright colors
to welcome spring.
And in Portugal,
they throw flour on
someone for an April
Fools' joke. Iran may
have the oldest joke day
ever. They go on picnics, then throw
away all the green vegetables to keep
away bad luck."

"No more spinach,"
said Frank, pretend-
tossing it over his
shoulder.

"In Scotland,
they have Hunt-the-
Cuckoo Day."

7

"That's cuckoo!" said Judy.

"On that day, you send somebody on a fool's errand."

"What's a fool's errand?" asked Frank.

"It's like a pretend trip or a wild-goose chase. Say I sent you down to fourth grade to deliver a message, but there was no real message."

Jessica Finch raised her hand.

"Question?" asked Mr. Todd.

"Comment," said Jessica. "My dad played an April Fools' joke on me. You know how I like pink? And pigs? While I was asleep, he took all the pink stuff out of my room. And all the pigs, too. When I woke up, my whole room was green and full of frogs."

"That's a good one," said Mr. Todd.

Frank told about the time his sister drew an April Fools' mustache on him while he was sleeping. And Judy laughed about putting a fake ice cube (with a dead fly in the middle of it) in Stink's glass of water.

"Did you ever have an April Fools' joke played on you, Mr. Todd?" Judy asked.

"Stor-y! Stor-y!" chanted Class 3T.

Mr. Todd glanced at the clock. "We have time for one story before we leave for Library class. Let's see. There was one time when I was a student teacher . . ."

"Tell us!"

"My sixth-graders played a prank on me, and got me good."

"Did they put gummy worms in your apple?"

"It was something worse than gummy worms," said Mr. Todd.

"Did they make you toothpaste Oreos?" somebody asked.

"Something worse," said Mr. Todd.

"Did they face their desks backward?"

"No, no, and nope. Ready for this?

During recess, they phoned to have a bunch of pizzas delivered to our class!"

Class 3T let out a gasp.

"The pizza guy showed up with a stack of pizza boxes as tall as the Leaning Tower of Pisa. I told him it had to be a mistake. That's when the whole class yelled, 'April Fools'!'"

"What did you do?"

"What could I do? I paid for the pizzas . . . and we had an April Fools' pizza party!"

"Can we do that?" asked Frank.

"I think not," said Mr. Todd.

But Mr. Todd's story gave Judy an idea. A best-ever brainstorm. She, Judy Moody, would play an April Fools' joke on Mr. Todd.

After all, they were learning about April Fools' Day. Thinking up a joke to play on Mr. Todd would be like homework. And pranking him on April Fools' Day would be extra credit!

CHAPTER 2
Oodles of Moodles

After school, Judy was making a
WORLD'S BEST TEACHER poster for
Mr. Todd's new bulletin board.

"Stink," said Judy, "help me think
up a joke. I want to play an April
Fools' joke on Mr. Todd."

"No way can you play an April
Fools' joke on your *teacher*," said
Stink. "Your *teacher* makes your report
card, remember?"

"Then help me think up a way-funny, A-plus joke."

"Whoopee cushion?" asked Stink.

"Too embarrassing," said Judy.

"Fake hand?" asked Stink. "You could put it in his desk."

Judy chewed on her pencil. "What else have you got?"

"Exploding gum?" said Stink.

"No gum in school."

"I got it!" Stink pointed to Judy's poster. "Cross out World's BEST Teacher and change it to World's WORST Teacher." He cracked himself up.

"That joke gets a D-minus, Stink," said Judy. "An April Fools' joke has to make you laugh, not hurt your feelings."

"For real?" said
Stink.

"Did it hurt
your feelings
when I put blue
milk in your
cereal? Or hid a

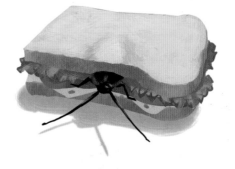

plastic cockroach
in your sandwich?
Or got you to
believe that our
mailman, Jack
Frost, was from

the North Pole?"

"That was
funny!" said Stink.

"I rest my case,"
said Judy.

The next morning, Judy woke up
in a good mood, even though she still
did not have a joke to play on Mr.
Todd.

"Happy April Fools' Day, Mouse!"

Judy ran downstairs. Sitting on
the table was a lumpy present from
Stink. *Hel-lo!* She, Judy Moody, had a
birthday today. No fooling.

"Happy Birthday, Jelly Bean," said Dad.

Mom kissed Judy right on top of her messy hair. "Happy Birthday!"

"Wait for me!" said Stink, sliding into the room on sock feet. "I want to watch you open your present from me. It's something you want really bad."

"It's pretty small for a puppy," said Judy.

"Guess again!" said Stink. "But it is from Fur & Fangs."

"A two-toed sloth? A sugar glider?"

"Open it!"

Judy tore off the paper. It was not a two-toed sloth. It was not a sugar glider. It was . . . nothing but a stick. An ugly, skinny, brown stick inside a plastic critter case.

Wait just a creepy-crawly second!

The stick had legs! Skinny brown toothpick legs. And the stick moved!

"Ooh. A bug that looks exactly like a stick!"

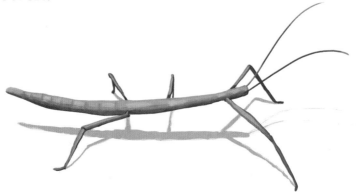

"It's an Indian walking stick. Nickname: Franken-stickie," said Stink. "I wanted to get you a Goliath walking stick. A Goliath is almost as long as *two* rulers, but it cost twenty-two dollars. This one was on sale because it's missing a leg. But it'll grow back. You'll see."

Judy nodded. "Thanks, Stinkbug. I think I'm going to name it Twiggy! I can't wait to show Rocky and Frank and Mr. Todd—"

Mr. Todd! Wait just a stick-bug-not-stink-bug minute! She, Judy Moody, Birthday Girl, had just come up with the best April Fools' joke ever!

At the bus stop, Judy collected sticks and put them in the critter case with Twiggy. She had pencils that looked like twigs and she added those, too.

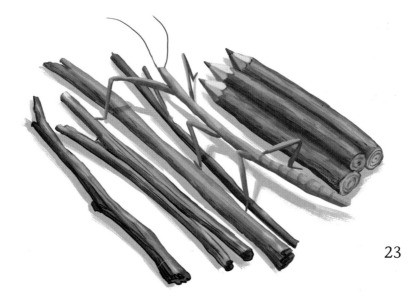

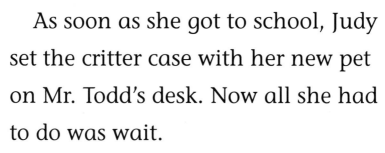

As soon as she got to school, Judy set the critter case with her new pet on Mr. Todd's desk. Now all she had to do was wait.

Let the April Fooling begin!

"Good morning, class. Happy April Fools' Day," said Mr. Todd. He spied the critter case. "Ho! What's this? Sticks?"

"It's Judy Moody's," said Jessica.

"You know how I collect Band-Aids and scabs and junk?" said Judy. "Sticks are my new thing."

Mr. Todd just shook his head. He wrote *Rhyme Time* on the board. "In England, if you get an April Fools' joke played on you, they call you a noodle. Who can give me a word that rhymes with *noodle*?"

"*Poodle!*" called Jessica.

"That's using your noodle." Mr. Todd turned to write on the board.

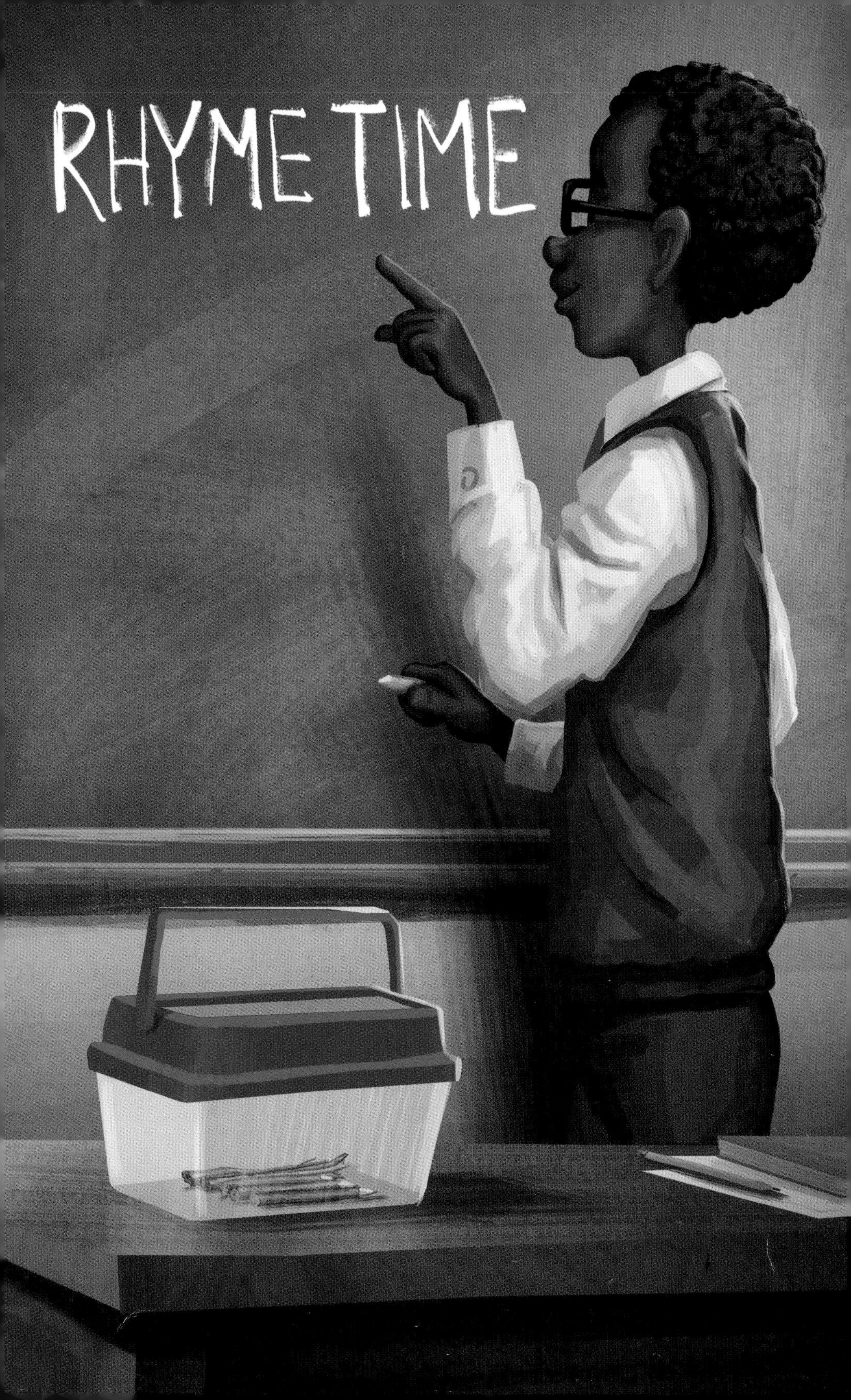
RHYME TIME

"Hey!" said Jessica. "One of Judy's sticks moved!"

Not now, Twiggy. Not yet.

Mr. Todd peered at the stick collection. Nothing. Twiggy did not move one toothpick leg.

Mr. Todd turned back to the board.

"Oodle!" "Kaboodle!"

Judy doodled in her notebook.

"Any more words that rhyme with *noodle*?" Mr. Todd asked.

"Doodle!" called Judy.

"Hey, see?" said Jessica, pointing. "One of Judy's sticks moved again . . . all by itself."

Mr. Todd turned back around. But Twiggy was hiding under the lid now.

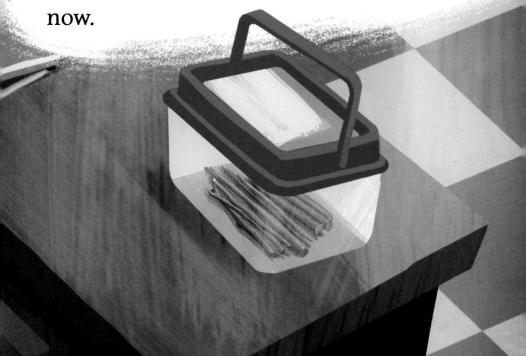

Phew. When Mr. Todd wasn't looking, Twiggy was on the move. But every time the teacher turned around, Twiggy was stick-still.

Mr. Todd wrote *moodle* on the board.

"*Moodle* is not a word," said Jessica Finch.

"Sure it is," said Mr. Todd. "A moodle is what you call a little mood."

"Oh," said Jessica.

"April Fools'!" said Mr. Todd. Everybody cracked up. Mr. Todd turned back to the board.

Just then, Judy saw two antennae poke up through the top of the critter case. *No, Twiggy, you little sneaker-doodle.* Then a toothpick leg popped up, then another, and before you could say "Oodles of poodles," Twiggy had crawled right up out of the critter case.

Uh-oh!

She, Judy Moody, was in a moodle.

Jessica Finch jumped out of her seat. "Told you! That stick! It's aliiiive!"

Twiggy inched across a stack of math homework. Twiggy crept up the back of Mr. Todd's chair. Twiggy raced up Mr. Todd's sleeve and crawled right up . . .

"Mr. Todd! It's on your head!" yelled Jessica Finch.

Mr. Todd plucked the stick from his hair and held it in his hand.

"April Fools'!" Judy yelled. "It's not a stick. It's a stick *bug*. Meet Twiggy, my new pet. She's an Indian walking stick."

"Look at that," said Mr. Todd, peering at the bug over his glasses. He held it up for the class to see. "It really does look just like a stick. Isn't nature amazing?"

Class 3T *ooh*ed and *aah*ed over Twiggy.

"Did I fool you?" Judy asked Mr. Todd.

"A-plus! You got me good," said Mr. Todd. "But you'd better watch out, Judy Moody. I might have a trick or two up my sleeve. April Fools' Day isn't over yet."

Gulp!

"Mr. Todd," asked Judy, "what rhymes with *uh-oh*?"

CHAPTER 3
Mystery of the Missing Birthday

At lunch, Judy found a fake tomato slice in her peanut-butter-and-jelly sandwich. *Mom!* Hidden under her sandwich was a birthday five-dollar bill from Dad. NOT! It was fake money.

Rocky got a meatball cupcake in his lunch. When Frank tore open his bag of cheese doodles, there were healthy snacks inside—carrots! Frank snorted and chocolate milk went up his nose.

Amy Namey's pudding pack had googly eyes. Even Jessica Finch's bagel was made to look like a doughnut with sprinkles. But phony tomato slices, meatball cupcakes, and the Great Doughnut Fake-Out were nothing compared to what Mr. Todd might do to her.

Judy was full of itches and fidgets. How could she sit still as a stick bug when, any minute, Mr. Todd might throw flour on her, like in Portugal? Or write a big fat *F*-for-*Flunk* on her homework sheet? Or worse . . . send her to Antarctica (the desk in the back of the class) for no reason!

All afternoon, kids kept looking at her and giggling. "Hey, Rock," Judy said. "Do I have a fish on my back or something?" She twirled left. She twirled right. She reached behind her back and grabbed the piece of paper taped there.

"Shark!" said Judy. *Oh, that Mr. Todd.*

"April Fish!" yelled Frank.

"It's a Frank prank!" said Rocky. Judy cracked up. But the day was almost over, and Mr. Todd still had not played a trick on her. *Weird.*

Wait just a mini-cupcake minute! Judy had been so busy thinking about April Fools' Day that she almost forgot it was her birthday!

Judy looked around the room for any sign of a birthday. No silly hat in the shape of a cake. No giant Happy Birthday sunglasses. Judy's name was not even up on the board.

Even Nancy Drew couldn't solve the Mystery of the Missing Birthday. *Weird and weirder!*

Then it happened. Mr. Todd asked, "Who will go to the office and pick up a package for me?"

Package! Of course! The package had to be her very own class birthday present—a box of mini-cupcakes.

All hands shot up.

"Judy," said Mr. Todd.

Judy rushed down the hall to the principal's office. "Hi, Ms. Tuxedo!" she said to the principal. "I'm here to pick up a package for my birth—for Mr. Todd."

"Package? There's no package here, honey."

"A box? Pink maybe? Smells like cupcakes? Not meatball cupcakes. *Real* cupcakes."

"Sorry. No box and no cupcakes, meatball or otherwise."

Judy's heart sank. Mr. Todd had sent her on one of those fool's errands, and she was the noodle. No fair! *D-minus, Mr. Todd.*

Judy moped back to class. But when she got there, her class was missing! As in G-O-N-E *gone*.

"Anything wrong?" asked Ms. Tuxedo, coming up behind Judy.

"My class is missing!"

"A whole heap of third-graders can't just disappear," said Ms. Tuxedo. "Let's check the multi."

Judy followed Ms. Tuxedo to the multipurpose room, but it was dark. No Mr. Todd, no Class 3T in there.

Suddenly, the lights came on. The curtain on the stage opened.

"Surprise!" sang Mr. Todd.

"April Fools'!" shouted Class 3T.

Each kid in Judy's class was holding a piece of cardboard with a letter drawn on it. One by one they stepped forward, until Judy could read:

Mr. Todd had not forgotten her birthday after all.

"Surprised?" asked Mr. Todd.

Judy nodded. "This was *your* idea?"

"With a little help from the class," said Mr. Todd. He held out a pink box full of mini-cupcakes. "And your mom and dad."

"A-plus, Mr. Todd. You got me so good," said Judy. "I was sure you all forgot my birthday and went to Antarctica or something."

"Or something!" yelled Rocky and Frank.

"Rare!" said Judy. She took a mega-bite of her not-meatball mini-cupcake. "Best April Fools' joke ever."

"Judy, would you like to be first to get your face painted?" a voice said.

The voice belonged to Ms. Tater. Ms. Tater was an artist and Mr. Todd's girlfriend and she had written a book about crayons.

"Ms. Tater-Tot!" said Judy. "Oops, I mean Ms. Tater. Did you come to talk to our class about crayons?"

Ms. Tater laughed. "Not this time. Mr. Todd invited me. I thought I'd brighten up your birthday with a little face-painting."

April Fish and spaghetti trees!

"Just like in India," said Judy.

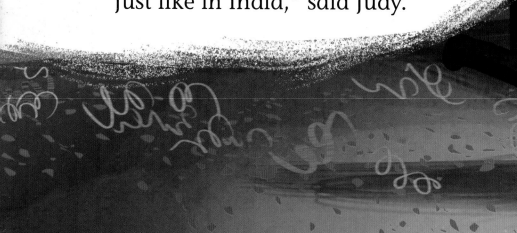

Ms. Tater held out her paintbrush. "What will it be? A butterfly? A balloon? A birthday cake?"

"A Band-Aid, of course," said Judy, pointing to her cheek.

After face-painting, it was picture time. Class 3T crowded in front of a spaghetti tree they had made out of cardboard and paper. Oodles of wiggly noodles hung from the branches.

Judy put on the birthday-cake hat and the giant Happy Birthday sunglasses.

"Say cheese!" said Mr. Todd.

"April Fish and spaghetti trees!" said Judy, grinning like an April fool.